CW00811306

CHART HITS
easy playalong *for* flute

WISE PUBLICATIONS
London/New York/Paris/Sydney/Copenhagen/Madrid/Tokyo

Exclusive Distributors:
Music Sales Limited
8/9 Frith Street,
London W1D 3JB, England.

Music Sales Pty Limited
120 Rothschild Avenue,
Rosebery, NSW 2018,
Australia.

Order No. AM967780
ISBN 0-7119-8539-1
This book © Copyright 2001 by Wise Publications.

Music arranged by CN Productions Ltd.
Music processed by Enigma Music Production Services.
Cover photography courtesy George Taylor.
Printed in the United Kingdom by
Printwise (Haverhill) Limited, Haverhill, Suffolk.

CD engineered by Arthur Dick.
Instrumental solos by John Whelan.

Your Guarantee of Quality:
As publishers, we strive to produce every book to
the highest commercial standards.
The music has been freshly engraved and the book
has been carefully designed to minimise awkward page
turns and to make playing from it a real pleasure.
Particular care has been given to specifying acid-free,
neutral-sized paper made from pulps which have not
been elemental chlorine bleached.
This pulp is from farmed sustainable forests and
was produced with special regard for the environment.
Throughout, the printing and binding have been planned
to ensure a sturdy, attractive publication which should
give years of enjoyment.
If your copy fails to meet our high standards,
please inform us and we will gladly replace it.

Music Sales' complete catalogue describes
thousands of titles and is available in full colour
sections by subject, direct from Music Sales Limited.
Please state your areas of interest and send
a cheque/postal order for £1.50 for postage to:
Music Sales Limited, Newmarket Road,
Bury St. Edmunds, Suffolk IP33 3YB.

www.musicsales.com

Junior Guest Spot

Flute Fingering Chart

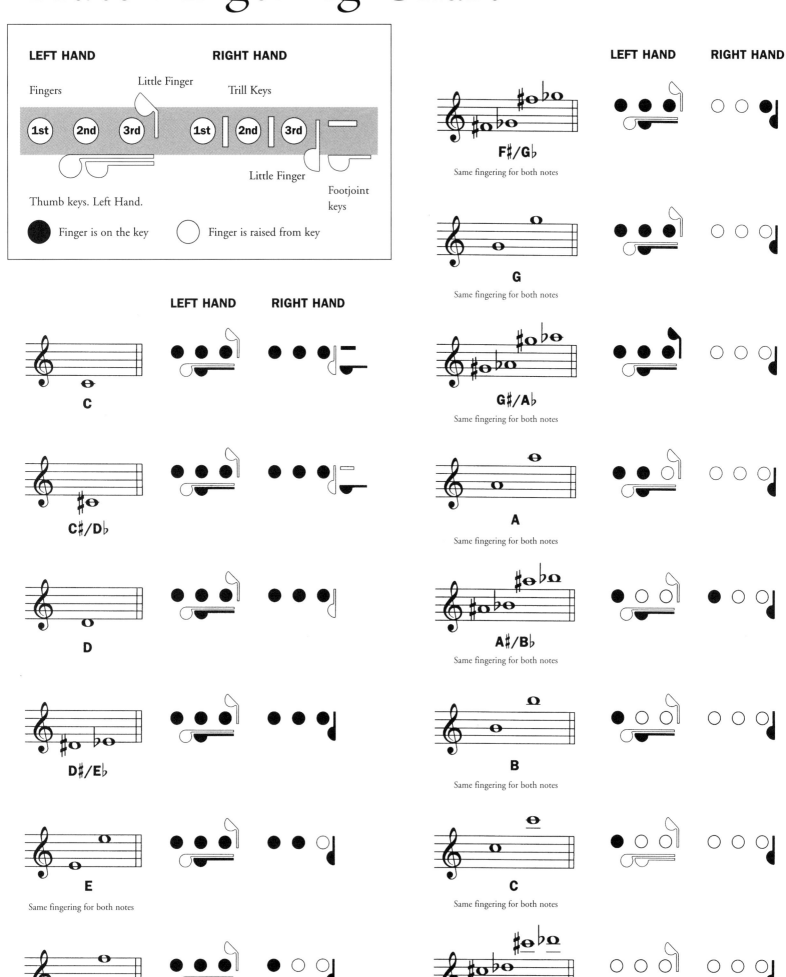

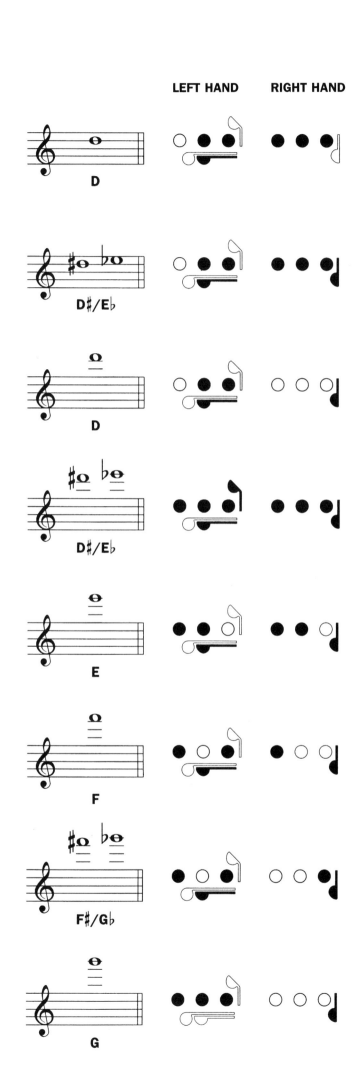

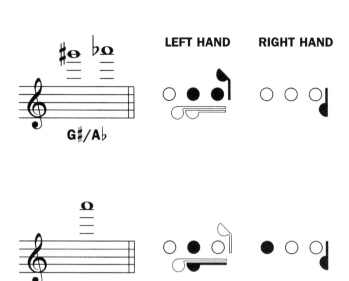

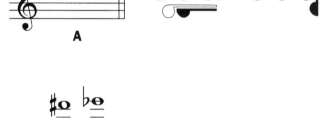

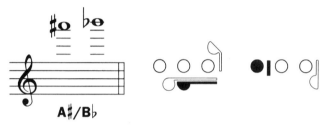

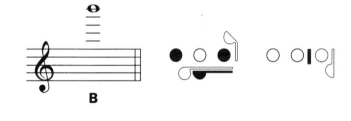

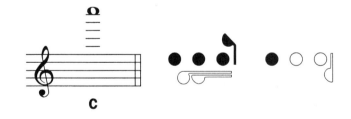

AMERICAN PIE

Words & Music by Don McLean

both kicked off your shoes_ man I dig those rhy - thm and blues._ I was a

lone - ly teen - age bronc - in' buck with a pink car - na - tion and a

pick - up truck. But I knew that I was out___ of luck the day_

__ the mu - sic died. I start - ed sing - ing

bye - bye Miss A - me - ri - can Pie._ Drove my che - vy to the lev - ee but the

lev - ee was dry._ Them good ole boys_were drink - in' whis - ky and rye_ sing - in'

"This will be the day that I die. This will be the day that I die."

We start - ed sing - ing_____ we start - ed sing - ing_____

we start - ed sing - ing_____ we start - ed sing - ing._____

BLACK COFFEE

Words & Music by Tom Nichols, Alexander Soos & Kirsty Elizabeth

BREATHLESS

Words & Music by R. J. Lange, Andrea Corr, Caroline Corr, Sharon Corr & Jim Corr

Moderately

IT FEELS SO GOOD

Words & Music by Sonique, Linus Burdick & Simon Belofsky

MY LOVE

Words & Music by Jörgen Elofsson, Pelle Nylén, David Kreuger & Per Magnusson

An emp-ty street an emp-ty house, a hole in-side my heart. I'm all a-lone, the rooms are get-ting small-er. I won-der how, I won-der why, I won-der where they are. The days we had, the songs we sang to-ge-ther. And oh, my love, I'm hold-ing on for-ev-er, reach-ing for a love that seems so far. So I say a lit-tle prayer and hope my dreams will take me there, where the skies are blue to see you once a-gain my love.__ O-ver

seas from coast to coast to find the place I love the most. Where the

fields are green to see you once a - gain___ to hold you in my

arms to pro - mise you my love to tell you from the

heart you're all I'm think-ing of. I'm

reach - ing for a love that seems so far. So, so I

say a lit - tle prayer and hope my dreams will take me there. Where the

skies are blue, to see you once a - gain my love___ o - ver

seas, from coast to coast, to find the place I love the most. Where the

fields are green, to see you once a - gain. My love.___

NATURAL BLUES

Words by Vera Hall
Music by Vera Hall & Moby
'Natural Blues' is based on the song 'Trouble So Hard' (Words & Music by Vera Hall)

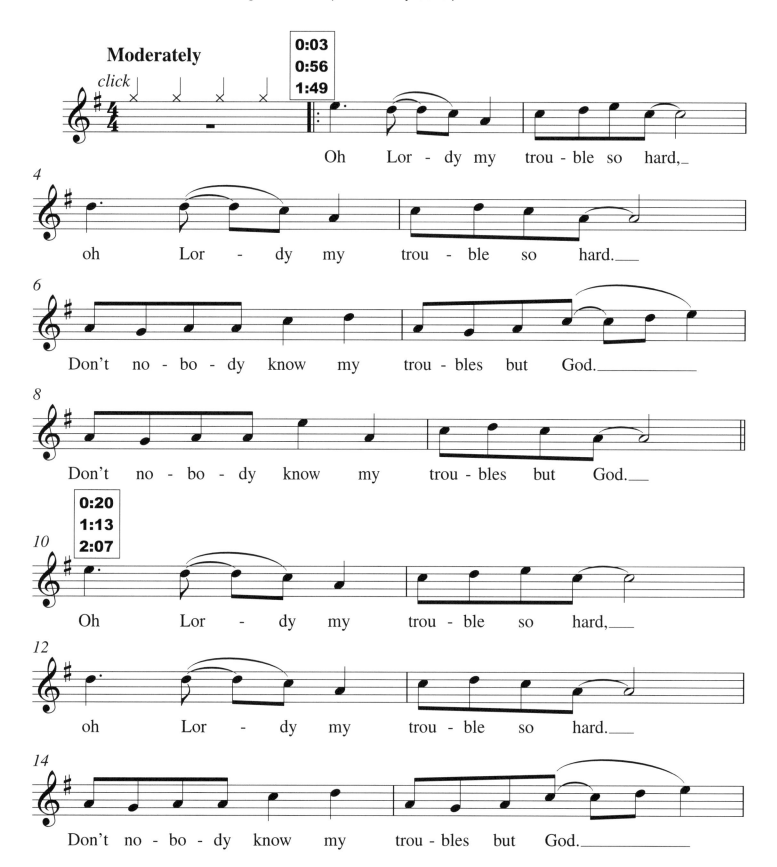

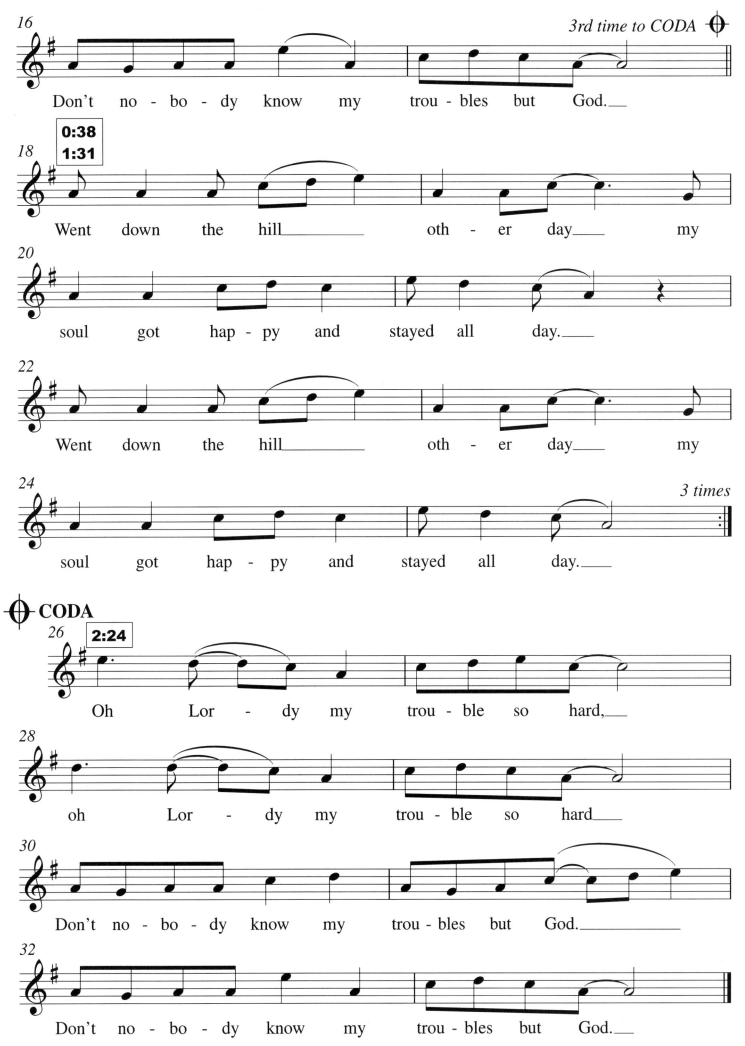

REACH

Words & Music by Cathy Dennis & Andrew Todd

RISE

Words & Music by Bob Dylan, Gabrielle, Ferdy Unger-Hamilton & Ollie Dagois

SHAPE OF MY HEART

Words & Music by Max Martin, Rami & Lisa Miskovsky

STOMP

Words & Music by Mark Topham, Karl Twigg & Rita Campbell

STRONGER

Words & Music by Max Martin & Rami

SUPREME

Words & Music by Robbie Williams, Guy Chambers, Dino Fekaris & Frederick Perren

WALKING AWAY

Words & Music by Craig David & Mark Hill

THE WAY YOU MAKE ME FEEL

Words & Music by Phil Thornalley & Bryan Adams

I'M OUTTA LOVE

Words & Music by Anastacia, Sam Watters & Louis Biancaniello

Moderately fast

Now ba-by come on___ don't claim that love you

nev-er let me feel._ I should haveknown, ___ 'cause you've brought no-thing

real._ Come on, be a man_ a-bout it. You won't die_ I ain't got no more

tears to cry and I can't_ take this no more._ You know I got - ta let it

go. And you know_ I'm out-ta love,___ set me free and let me out_

— of this mi - se - ry.___ Just show me the way_ to get my life a- gain,___

you can't han-dle me. Said I'm out-ta love_ can't you see, ba-by it's you_

1. **2.**

— got-ta set_ me free._ I'm out-ta love___ I'm out-ta love_ ___

12/03 (49833)